Pirate Treasure Ahoy!

Nicholas Pavitt

by Nicholas Pavitt

Copyright © 2015 Nicholas Pavitt

Cover design, text and illustrations by Nicholas Pavitt.

ISBN-10: 1518827721

ISBN-13: 978-1518827723

1

Jolly Roger, the Pirate Captain, called his crew onto the sunny deck of his beloved ship, *The Golden Shark*. Waiting nervously, the pirate crew wondered what this could mean: Was the captain angry? Did he have news for them? Or were they about to chase another ship?

"Shipmates," growled Jolly Roger, "I 'ave 'ere a treasure map, and at sunrise tomorrow we'll begin the search for this 'ere Treasure Island!"

Imagining the shiny treasure they might find, the pirate crew began to cheer.

3

The next day a fisherman spotted the *The Golden Shark* sailing towards the coast of Hatland. He raced to warn the other Hatpeople that the pirates were approaching. Fear quickly spread from village to village, as messages were sent to the castle to warn the King and Queen.

As news reached the castle, the King and Queen paced up and down thinking of what could be done to protect Hatland.

The Queen called for Hatricks the magician, but, looking into his crystal ball and seeing the pirate ship on the sea, he replied, "I'm afraid long-distance magic is just too dangerous!"

"I thought so," remarked the King, "I know, let's call for the navy's Captain Nell!"

Captain Nell arrived to a fanfare at the castle, and calmly stood before the King and Queen.

"Captain Nell, you've heard about the pirate ship?" asked the Queen.

"Yes, Your Majesty," replied Captain Nell, "my ship HMS *Seahorse* is ready to sail."

"Good," said the King, "your orders are to sink or capture that pirate ship as quickly as possible."

"Aye-aye!" replied Captain Nell as she started to race off.

"Just one moment," called Hatricks, "I'll give you something to help your mission."

"Here we go again!" muttered the Queen and King under their breath.

With a wave of his wand a large magical feather appeared in a flash!

"Err, thank you," said a baffled Captain Nell, grabbing the feather as she disappeared out of the castle and across the drawbridge towards her ship.

At the wheel of HMS *Seahorse*, Captain Nell found the magical feather twitched this way and that, pointing to where the pirate ship sailed over the sea ahead.

"Ship ahoy!" called a sailor from high in the masts after days of sailing, and with her trusty telescope Captain Nell could see the pirate ship, *The Golden Shark*, on the horizon.

Jolly Roger's parrot spotted Captain Nell's ship and began to squawk, "Ship Ahoy! Ship Ahoy!" Jolly Roger turned *The Golden Shark* to face Captain Nell's ship, as if to attack!

At this moment, the gigantic arms of a sea monster rose out of the sea and began to grab at the pirate ship. *The Golden Shark* rocked to one side, and the pirates fell over onto the deck and Jolly Roger's parrot flapped and squawked, "Trouble! Trouble!" as it flew over to HMS *Seahorse*.

"Save us! Save us!" squawked Jolly Roger's parrot to Captain Nell.

Captain Nell thought.

"Just sink them!" called out her sailors.

Captain Nell replied, "No, they have not done anything wrong."

With that, an idea flashed into Captain Nell's head.

"Take this magic feather, you know what to do," she said as she gave the magic feather to the parrot.

The parrot flew with the magic feather in its beak over to the pirate ship, where the sea monster kept grabbing at more of the ship.

The parrot swooped down and tickled the arms of the sea monster with the magic feather and, arm by arm, the ticklish sea monster let go of the ship and slowly returned to the deep sea.

Jolly Roger thanked Captain Nell for saving the pirates and their ship.

"I think it was your parrot that did the saving," replied Captain Nell.

Jolly Roger explained that he had a treasure map and the pirates were only searching for the Treasure Island.

"I've an idea," said Captain Nell, "we'll help you find the treasure and we'll share it."

"It's a deal," agreed Jolly Roger.

Day after day, the two ships sailed in search of the Treasure Island, the magic feather twitching this way and that, North, East, South and West.

"Island ahoy! Island ahoy!" squawked the parrot returning from a flight, and there slowly appeared before them an island with mountains and a smoking volcano, just as on the treasure map.

Onto the beach, up a path in the cliff, over grassland and through a forest the pirates and sailors followed Jolly Roger, leading the way across the island with the map.

And then they crossed some more grassland, and marched through a very similar forest.

"I think we should have brought the magic feather with us," said a glum Captain Nell taking the map and leading the way. "It might have done better than your map-reading Jolly Roger! You are taking us in circles!"

Out of the forest they marched and then Captain Nell and her sailors began to sink, slowly, into a swamp.

"Help!" they cried, "Help! Help!"

Using all of their might, Jolly Roger and his pirates pulled Captain Nell and her sailors out of the swamp.

"Now look who's not reading the map properly!" growled Jolly Roger.

"Thank you," replied Captain Nell wiping mud off her nose. "Okay, let's stop and take a closer look at the map."

"Yes, look, as I thought, the treasure is on the beach beyond the swamp," said Captain Nell.

"Aye, but you're not supposed to go THROUGH the swamp!" laughed Jolly Roger.

Onwards they marched, past waterfalls with shimmering rainbows, towards where the treasure was shown on the map.

"X marks the spot!" shouted Captain Nell and Jolly Roger together as they stood on the beach beneath palm trees with sand glimmering all around them in the sunlight.

But, where exactly was X on the beach? Hole after hole the pirates and sailors dug, but no treasure could be found.

Suddenly, out of nowhere, the magic feather appeared, but was snatched away by a gust of wind. The parrot flew after the feather, through the palm trees and into a cave, as everybody followed trying to catch it.

There in the cave the pirates and sailors found the treasure!

In the cave stood an empty treasure chest , with jewels glistening and sparkling in the walls of the cave all around!

"Wonderful!" gasped Jolly Roger.

"Fantastic!" agreed Captain Nell.

"Right, let's dig them out and fill the chest!" called Jolly Roger to his pirates.

"No," said Captain Nell in the sparkling light, "keep the wonder here for others to find too. I think we've found a treasure far greater than gold, silver and jewels - friendship!"

As the sun set far out to sea the pirates and sailors celebrated singing sea-shanties and dancing on the beach.

The King and Queen watched the celebration in Hatricks' crystal ball knowing all Hatland was safe and the world was full of wonder and adventure. 24